The Four

O

Anthony Goulet

This book is dedicated to you.

Preface

Eight years have passed since *The Four* was published. And almost eleven years have passed since *The Four* was written. When I sat down to write *The Four*, I wrote about characters who comprise all human beings - all life. Characters such as Love, Prayer, Laughter, Tears, Remember, Dreams, Vision, Purpose and You. These are characters beyond characters; they are the deeper truths that unify us, truths we must return to for our own well-being and the well-being of all life.

I wrote *The Four* when I was working full-time as a street-level Gang Interventionist. I was desperately tired of seeing youth and young adults hurt and kill one another over perceived differences. My work then was, and still is today, building bridges and walking others back to all the beauty that unifies us - all the beauty that *is* us. One evening, I returned home late from some street-level interventions. Echoing in my mind were the bloodcurdling screams of a parent who had lost her child to violence on the streets, the last words her child said to me, and the sound of automatic gunfire. I fell to my knees, cried, and begged the Creator for an answer to share. I went to sleep. And when I woke up, I was gifted with the first thread of the story that is *The Four*. I held on to that thread, prayed, got out of the way, and allowed Spirit to weave *The Four* through me.

The Four is more than just a story. It is an answer the Creator poured through me, which is why this book is dedicated to *you*. If you take the time to read this short book, no matter where you are and no matter what you are going through or have gone through, this book will help you return to the answers that have always been within you.

I decided to relaunch *The Four* in a larger book format to make the reading experience more enjoyable. But mostly I relaunched *The Four* because taking the sacred walk from our heads back to our hearts to reclaim our vision, mission, dreams and purpose is real, important, possible, and more necessary now than ever before.

May the Creator bless you and your family.

Walk in Beauty – Walk in Love,

Anthony Goulet

realwarriorslove@realwarriorslove.com

April 2021

The Four

Love, Prayer, Laughter and Tears are *The Four*. They grew up together. They were all they knew. Side by side and in complete unison, they danced through the best and the worst life had to offer. More impressive than how they handled what life offered them is what they offered life. Their unified presence transformed the very fabric of life. The synergy that moved through and with these four best friends prompted the mountains to bow and reminded the stars why they shine. In their presence the sun and moon knew no distance between one another. Their company made time meaningless, yet reminded others what time is for. The truest and deepest relationship is what they experienced together, and allowed all those in their presence to experience the same.

They shared their entire childhood and adolescence together at their favorite restaurant and the park across the street from the restaurant. At the restaurant they filled themselves and one another with delicious food, joy, and dialogue that was entrancing to all who sat near their table. After filling themselves and the restaurant with life, they would walk across the street to the park where they would sing, write, paint, draw, dance, and engage everyone in a bliss that was nothing less than miraculous, and nothing more than a peace offering to all who happened to be in the park while the Four were there. People gathered at the restaurant and park

1

because of the Four. Their presence made everyone's food taste better, the park greener, the joy deeper, and the experience richer. The stress from a long day dissolved when the Four entered any space, so it was with great expectation many longed for the Four's continued company.

Four years have passed since Love, Prayer, Laughter and Tears were all together. Like children playing in the water on a hot summer day, allowing majestic rainbows to manifest upon their hands, Love, Prayer, Laughter and Tears held the greatest relationship but did not hold on to it. The last time they were together was different. They ate together at the restaurant but did not talk as much. They were polite but not truthful. All of them in their own way knew they would be parting ways, but none dared to speak of it. The meal was spent like squeezing a dried lemon, attempting to get a drop of happiness out of that moment, but there was none. They filled in the truth they were unable to speak with small talk. Underneath the small talk contained what each of them was concealing from themselves and each other. What they were holding back was the very reason they were holding back. Before they had the ability to let go of one another, they each first let go of themselves. It was the first time they did not follow the voice they knew - their own sacred, unified voice. They separately listened to, believed, and began to follow the

2

voices of strangers. Strangers who consistently and persuasively told them they each needed to go become something and somebody. Until that day, they each knew they were already something, already somebody, and much more than just some bodies. Love was told she was vulnerable and needed to protect herself. Prayer was told he was unrealistic and needed to become practical. Laughter was told she was immature and needed to become sophisticated. Tears was told he was weak and needed to stay inside to become strong.

At the Four's last meal together those whose dreams and inspirations ignited in their presence recognized something was wrong. The unspoken, yet obvious shift within the Four, shifted everyone in their presence back to what the Four were feeling for the first time, fragmented. It was the first time the Four knew piece, not peace. No one knew exactly what happened, not even the Four, but it reverberated through everyone they encountered that day. The restaurant's owner and patrons noticed the once vibrant and illuminating group now looked more like four acquaintances having a casual business meeting. The patrons commented to one another about their shared disappointment but said nothing to the Four. The restaurant's owner and patrons yearned for the joy the Four normally infiltrated the restaurant with. Patrons

3

began to leave because it was not just the food they were there for. Some went to the park across the street hoping the Four would make their way there as they usually did. Those who waited at the park were disenchanted because the Four did not go to the park that day. How could they? They did not have anything to write, paint, sing, or draw. After their meal they each politely hugged one another and went on their separate journeys to attain what the voices of strangers told them they needed.

For four years each one walked countless journeys in search of what they were told they needed to not be deficient. Being astute in the learning process, the Four understood the importance of first emptying themselves to be filled with new insights and better ways of being. Before embarking on their separate journeys, they each laid down their tools to make room for the new ones they would receive. Before leaving on her quest to find invulnerability, Love laid down forgiveness. As soon as Love laid it down, she experienced something she had never felt before, pain. It was a pain that penetrated deeply into her very being. Believing the voice that told her she was vulnerable, she assumed the pain was confirmation of her vulnerability.

Prayer laid down hope. When he laid it down it was the first time he experienced discouragement. Considering the voice

4

who told him he needed to be realistic, Prayer assumed discouragement to be part of what he must accept to become realistic.

Laughter set aside joy and immediately felt sorrow. Believing the voice that told her she needed to be sophisticated, she interpreted sorrow as a sign of her first steps toward maturity.

Tears set aside compassion and instantly felt indifference. Although it was painful for him, he accepted this as evidence of his weakness the strangers' voice had told him about. He was on his way to not feeling and thought these were his first steps toward finding true strength.

Leaving behind the relationships and tools they knew, they separately traveled throughout the world. Within the towns, cities, coasts and villages, each encountered many other voices that reinforced the voices of the strangers which placed them on their separate journeys. Each of the Four met many individuals who were learning and practicing unforgiveness, discouragement, sorrow and indifference. Some were novices like them. Others were highly advanced apprentices. There were many more masters than any of them expected to encounter. In every place they learned more and were taught how to cultivate their new tools to become invulnerable, realistic, mature and strong. In every place where they lived and learned, there were also the mad ones.

The mad ones were those who the masses of masters considered to be insane. When the Four first began their journeys, the mad ones were those who Love, Prayer, Laughter and Tears saw something familiar in and were attracted to. After enough instances of the masses instructing the Four to not socialize with the mad ones, the Four learned to perceive the mad ones the same way the masses did. With time and relentless instruction from the masters, the Four were dedicated to their paths and eventually no longer entertained exploring their silly, indescribable familiarities with madmen and madwomen. The more the Four studied, practiced and shared their new tools with everyone they encountered, the more they were embraced by the masses. The acceptance of the masses was a place where they found solace. Their newfound solace was especially helpful to each of them when they tried to sleep. Anticipation of the embracement of the masses the following day was something they focused on while lying in bed. They each did this to counteract their nightly thoughts about where they came from and what they left behind.

In a short time, the pain from the tools of unforgiveness, discouragement, sorrow and indifference grew more intense within each of the Four. As their pain increased, the masters readily supplied them with justifications and reasoning that enhanced their tolerance. They were taught they were experiencing growing pains. The masters explained as with any tool, the more you use it, the more calluses you build and the easier the tools become to hold and use. Each of the Four reached a pivotal moment on their journeys when they questioned the soundness of their decisions, the voices they were following, and the masters they were learning from. This moment arose when the acceptance of the masses, justifications, reasoning, and calluses were not enough to alleviate the pain their new paths created within them. As each one of them reached this point the masters introduced them to the numbing agents. They were each taught the subtle and not-so-subtle ways of how to numb themselves from the torment their new, important and necessary tools provided. Once they accepted and used the numbing agents, they no longer questioned the voices of the strangers they followed or the masters they learned from. They became fully dedicated to applying their new tools, justifications, building more calluses and consuming numbing agents. Although none of the Four necessarily felt alive, this routine became their lives for four long years.

After a full day of practicing the arts of selfishness and unforgiveness within a city, Love was making her way back to an apartment she was renting. Along the way she was about to stop by a place where they sold numbing agents for a cheap price. As Love approached the door, she heard a voice whisper, "Hey." Love looked to her left where she saw one of the city's madmen standing in the alley. Disgusted by his mere presence, and even more so with the thought he may actually be speaking to her, Love probed, "Are you speaking to me?"

"Of course, I'm speaking to you," said the madman with a certainty only the mad enjoy.

Embarrassment consumed her as she quickly thought about what others would think if they saw her speaking to the madman. Love ignored him and took a step toward the door to enter the place where numbing agents were sold. As Love reached for the doorknob, the madman, now with tears pouring down his face, yelled, "Don't do it. Please. I do not want money. I want something much more precious than that. I want five minutes of your time, nothing more."

Love withdrew her hand from the doorknob, stepped away from the door and approached the madman with a tool she learned on her travels. She glared at the madman. It was a glare she had used many times to intimidate others on her journey. With great irritation and her refined glare of intimidation, Love whispered, "Okay, Madman, you have one minute. But do not think I care about your tears or your situation. Before you speak, know that I understand your level of weakness even more than you do."

Through a sniffle, as he wiped the tears from his face, the madman agreed, "Yes, I know you understand my weakness, my tears and my situation much better than I do. That is exactly why I called out to you. But you need to understand I'm here to save your life."

"My life?"

"Yes, your life. I know this area better than anyone here. I would say I have been here forever but that is not true. I have been here almost forever. You didn't even read the sign above the door of the establishment you were about to enter, did you?"

Leaning around the corner from the alley, Love looked up above the door of the establishment and read the sign: *P.O.N.R. Club*. After reading the sign, not wanting anyone to see her interacting with one of the mad ones, Love placed herself back in the alley, leaned on the wall, shrugged her shoulders, and said, "Yeah, so?"

"You don't get it. P.O.N.R. stands for Point of No Return. The numbing agents they sell are beyond anything you have ever tried before. Yes, you are calloused. Yes, you are tough. But you are no longer strong enough to withstand what they sell inside those places. There have been many we have tried to talk with before they go inside the P.O.N.R. Clubs, but many won't listen, and no one comes out of those clubs."

"Hold on. Wait a minute." Love was processing what the madman had said. "Did you say I am no longer strong enough to withstand what they sell in there?"

"Correct."

"Who in the hell do you think you are?"

"Hell isn't where we find the answer to who we are, hell is where it's forgotten."

With mocking laughter Love said, "Whatever. For your information I am stronger than I have ever been. You also mentioned there have been many people *we've* tried to talk with."

"Yes, that's right."

"Number one, I don't know you. And number two, who is this *we* you speak of?"

The madman motioned down the alley with a nod of his head, "Look down at the end of the alley. See the metal barrel with the fire in it, and the two women and one man standing around it, keeping warm?"

"Yes."

"They, plus me, are the we I speak of. I would like you to meet them."

"You still haven't told me who you are?"

"Oh, my apologies. I should have introduced myself first, but I usually have to introduce myself last. My name is Remember. Please come visit with us for a moment and keep warm. No one will see you with us down there. If you do not like our company, all you have to do is walk away and go back to the numbing agents of your choice."

Love deliberated about the dangers of walking down to the end of an alley with Remember to meet his friends and stand by a fire. Love thought to herself, *what if he is right about the P.O.N.R. Clubs?* She decided to walk down the alley, not because she was particularly interested in Remember, his friends, or their fire, but because she felt a little vulnerable about it. She walked with him to prove to herself she was indeed invulnerable. Walking down the alley with Remember she noticed the bricks the alley walls were made of were not visible. Both sides of the alley walls were covered in papers and none of them were blank. There were newspapers, sheets of music, handwritten letters, typed letters, diplomas, articles, resumes, business plans, marriage certificates, birth certificates, promotions, screenplays and drawings. Further down the alley the walls smoothly transitioned from papers to photographs. There were photos of babies, birthday parties, weddings, graduations and anniversaries. Any joyous, monumental event you can think of, there was a picture of it on the alley walls. None of this disturbed Love, she was enjoying it. What did disturb her was that she felt comfortable making this walk down the alley with Remember to meet his friends. For a moment she felt a childlike curiosity and forgot to be invulnerable. The unexpected feeling of wonder upon Love frightened her, so she reminded herself to be tough again.

As Love approached the metal barrel that contained a beautiful fire which danced with radiant colors of gold, yellow and blue, she felt welcomed, but did not let her guard down. Remember's three friends came from around the barrel to give Love a hug. Remember stopped them, "She's not ready for that." Remember's three friends nodded their heads in agreement and went back to their places around the barrel, leaving plenty of room for Love to have her space. Remember and his friends said nothing while Love was standing five feet away from the barrel. The fire was crackling with a beautiful intensity as all their shadows danced upon the papers and photographs on the alley walls. Remember and his friends enjoyed the fire and simply allowed Love to decide for herself. Love was curious about the papers and the photographs on the walls but did not ask about them. Eventually, Love stepped forward and stood close to the fire. Peering in the barrel something startled her, so she quickly stepped back.

Remember saw what happened and chuckled, "You should have seen yourself."

"What? You think it's funny I was startled? Because I can show you a thing or two about…"

"No, no, no. I meant that literally. You should have looked longer and seen yourself more because you are beautiful."

"What are you talking about, Remember? I do not understand you. You asked for five minutes. I said I would give you one. We are way past what I promised and even what you asked for. So, who are these people and what do you want?"

"You are right. You have given more than you promised as you always used to. Allow me to introduce to you my dear friends, Dreams, Vision and Purpose."

Love scowled at them thinking, *this is a shoddy looking bunch*. Under her breath she mumbled, "I can't believe I'm entertaining this. I'm hanging out in an alley at night with four mad ones around a barrel."

Ignoring Love's obvious disdain of being in their presence, Remember inquired, "We introduced ourselves, what's your name?"

Leaning her head back as she rolled her eyes and readied herself to placate the conversation for just a moment longer before she walked away from the mad ones, panic struck at the core of Love's very being. "I'm…My name is…I work at…What's happening? What are you doing to me? What's going on with me?"

"Breathe deep, sister," said Purpose gently. Love looked Purpose in the eyes, and the sound of her voice echoed an ease within Love she had not experienced since her last meal with her best friends. Purpose continued, "That is why we did not want you walking into the P.O.N.R. Club. Because you would have forgotten it forever."

Never breaking contact with Purpose's eyes, and with great hesitance, Love stammered, "Would have forgotten what forever?"

"You would have forgotten your name, your real name. Do not be scared, honey. It is hard to say if you have not said it for a long time. What should concern you is never being able

14

to say it again. And that is what we are attempting to help you with."

"But I learned I don't need help. I've been working to become invulnerable."

Purpose nodded to Vision and because they work together so much, Vision fluidly added, "Help is a word used by the strong. Yes, you were taught to be strong means you do not need anyone, but this is simply not true. Being torn apart is the art of the great lie. The great lie is that anything real can be found apart from others, apart from creation. Truth, including true strength, is only found in remembering you are a part of everything not apart from anything. The great truth is whole, holiness, which is incapable of excluding anything real. Everything real is life, and life is all the great truth consists of. The great lie can only offer illusions. Illusions provide a perception, not a truth, that you can somehow be separate from life. Listening to, believing, and following the perception of the great lie is hell."

As it often does, the feeling of fear turned into anger and Love bellowed, "You're the mad ones living in the street. Look at you. You are living in ragged clothes, worn out, dirty, and nobody even likes you. If you are so smart and know so much about me, about life, then why aren't you all in better shape?"

Passionately, Dreams responded, "Because this is what happens to us after people forget their names. We huddle together. We keep one another warm. We live and continue to search for those who still have a light in their eyes, even if it is only a dim glimmer, and offer them a chance to evoke who they really are. We are all that comes out of the P.O.N.R. Clubs. Everyone thinks they walk inside those clubs alone, but we are inside everyone who enters those clubs."

"There was a time when we looked a lot different than we do now," explained Purpose. "We used to be sought after by everyone. We were well taken care of. That was a time before the numbing agents were introduced. Those times were so long ago I think only Remember remembers."

Remember gently placed his hand on Love's shoulder, "Please walk with me for a moment." Half in shock by all that transpired, Love did not hesitate and began to slowly stroll up the alley with Remember. As they walked, Remember expounded, "My friends and I are in every city, town, and village throughout the world. The name of this alley is *All That Never Got to Be*. This alley also exists in every city, town and village. Look at all these papers and photos. There are millions of them here. There are millions of them in every city, town and village. On these walls are all the graduations, marriages, birthdays, businesses, books, screenplays, songs, careers, loves, families and sweet memories that could have lived forever in the hearts and minds of those they were supposed to be shared with. All we can do is honor their memory and encourage others not to make the same mistake. Eventually, when my friends and I get everyone to evoke their real names, walking away from their true selves will be impossible. For every person who remembers their real name, a dream, purpose and vision are allowed back in, respected, nurtured and protected." As Love walked slowly up the alley with Remember she was in awe by his words and all that was on the walls. Making their way back toward the fire where Purpose, Dreams and Vision were waiting, Remember stopped and said, "It has to happen tonight. It is your choice. You can look in the fire, see your true self, remember your real name, say it out loud and reclaim it, or you can walk into the P.O.N.R. Club. Right now, you are halfway between the entrance of the P.O.N.R. Club and the fire. You are halfway between forgetting yourself forever or reclaiming yourself forever, but there is no middle ground after tonight."

Looking at Remember with a blank stare and with equally empty words, Love asked, "What if I don't do either tonight? What if I take a couple days and process all this? I understand what you are telling me. And I appreciate you showing me all of this, but this is overwhelming right now."

With a gentle smile, Remember emphasized, "You can do whatever you want, whenever you want to do it. But in the morning you will easily forget me and my friends. During the hustle and commotion of the day and the so-called masters of strength you will lose yourself forever, which will make it impossible to hear my voice call you again. Then you will enter the P.O.N.R. Club, and my friends and I will place all that your existence is supposed to bring forth on this wall."

"How do you know that? How can you be certain? Not everyone is alike. I know I'm stronger than many of the people on these walls."

"Yes, you are stronger than some on these walls and you are also weaker than others on these walls. How can I be certain? I can certainly tell you I have had this same conversation and listened to the same responses you are giving me, exactly the same number of times as there are papers and photographs on these walls. After tonight it's not that I won't call you again, but you won't hear me again. That is the point everyone gets to and you are at that point this evening. I will not interfere any longer. This is your process. You make your decision but I am going back with my friends. If you ever want to get back to your friends, you need to make the correct decision in this moment."

Hurling out the words through the instant tears that accompanied the thought of her friends, Love shouted, "Don't you bring up my friends, Remember. You don't even know my friends. And that's none of your business."

"That's exactly my business. You and your friends were led to your separate journeys by the voices of strangers. Sometimes, when accepted, the voice of a stranger can make a stranger of your own voice. Who is it that you think sparked the thoughts of your friends within you and the thoughts of you within your friends every evening since you all separated?"

"Okay, yes, I miss them, but everyone misses someone or something, don't they?"

"When you miss something or someone it is something or someone that is missing from you and you from them. Many have traveled great distances in search of truth and meaning. Even more have traveled greater distances to go back to a truth and meaning they once held, but for a myriad of reasons walked away from."

Leaving Love with that thought, Remember walked back and took his place around the fire with Dreams, Purpose and Vision. Love once again stood between two worlds. Unlike the journey she embarked upon four years ago, this time it was not someone or something telling her what she isn't and needs to become. It was a voice reminding her of what she is, calling her back. As painful as it was to try and become everything she never was, at that moment it felt just as painful to remember everything she forgot. Reflecting on what Remember and his friends reminded her of, she gazed at the walls and felt paralyzed. Within this paralysis she recognized that after all the work, calluses and practice she put into becoming what the masses of masters call strong, she would not be paralyzed if she had found true strength. She contemplated the possibility that her true strength must be in remembering, because the only place she had felt at ease in four years was by the fire with the mad ones. She decided to exercise true invulnerability by taking the walk of remembrance and took her place amongst Remember, Dreams, Vision and Purpose.

Standing by the metal barrel, Love first extended her hands toward the fire to warm herself. The warmth of the fire overtook her and instantly melted away the calluses she had developed, as well as the cold paralysis of insecurity. Love became soft again. In this softness she was once again what she had been seeking, strong. Only this time, she knew it. This true strength allowed Love to look into the fire and see herself. Looking deeply into the fire she observed the contour of her face, and then looked deeper. She saw the reflection of the fire in her eyes and her eyes in the fire. Within the dance of the fire she could see herself holding hands with Prayer, Laughter and Tears eating at the restaurant and playing in the park. Love smiled a smile of truth for the first time in four years. She called out her holy name, "I am Love. I am Love. I am Love." It echoed through the alley of All That Never Got to Be, and as she called her holy name the fourth time, "I am Love," it shook the Earth. Holding hands with Remember, Dreams, Purpose and Vision, Love reclaimed herself. Immediately after this great reclamation, Love knew she could not keep her strength up for long without her best friends. Love gave Remember, Dreams, Purpose and Vision hugs and thanked them profusely. Hurriedly, she told them, "I have to get back to the others because they need to remember as well. We need to remember together."

"You're correct," agreed Remember, "Get back to your friends and remind them. But know they have already heard your call. Love, please understand others hear you before they hear me, that is what made your particular case so crucial for all of us. You will understand what I mean by that very soon. Go on your way and find your friends. They need you and you need them."

21

United, Love, Prayer, Laughter and Tears held the power that literally made time stand still, yet the opposite occurred to them when they were separated. In four years, they each grew weak without the others. They each attempted to embrace what they were told to become with an expectation they would find who they really are. What they forgot is exactly what caused their separation. They forgot they never had to become anything because they were already everything. What Love discovered first with the help of Remember, Purpose, Dreams and Vision is there are roads that truly lead to nowhere. It is always counterintuitive to become something we are not. If we travel the road to nowhere far enough, it can also become counterintuitive to go back to who we are. After Love remembered, she knew she had to reach out to the others because she did not want her best friends to walk into a P.O.N.R. Club and forget themselves forever. Love rushed back to her apartment to make a call.

Walking past the P.O.N.R. Club back to the apartment she had been renting, all the people she passed were looking at her strangely. At first, Love felt uncomfortable with the stares from the masses until she realized what their strange looks were all about. It was the same nasty glares that Love, just hours before, had looked at the mad ones with. Happy to be on the receiving end of those looks instead of being contained within the pain that causes those looks, she lightly walked to her apartment, hurried to the telephone, and called Prayer. There was no ring, just silence after Love dialed Prayer's number.

"Hello. Prayer? This is Love."

"I know who this is. I called you but there was no ring. I dialed your number and heard you speak my name."

"No matter who called whom, it is just great to hear your voice, Prayer. How are you?"

"It has been an interesting evening to so say the least. I just got off the phone with Laughter and Tears who had nothing less than an interesting evening themselves."

"Let me guess. It had something to do with four friends and a P.O.N.R. Club, right?"

"Yes. It seems we all were fortunate enough to meet Remember, Purpose, Dreams and Vision."

"That is why I am calling you, Prayer. After my experience I really want all of us to meet at the park across the street from the restaurant. We must talk face to face. We just have to, and it cannot be delayed."

"We know, Love. I am leaving everything I accumulated on this journey here. I will be at the park in four days. Laughter and Tears are already on their way."

Feeling slightly excluded, a twinge of sadness came upon Love as she asked, "So you three were going to meet whether I was there or not?"

"Love, it is because of you that we are able to meet at all. All of us were going to walk inside different P.O.N.R. Clubs at the same time. None of us were listening to Remember, so we surely were not going to listen to his friends. We all had our hands on the doorknobs of those retched clubs, and Tears even had the door open. In the exact moment all of us were about to separately go inside forever, you said your holy name. The first time you called, we paused, thinking we were in a moment of weakness. The second time you called, we looked around for confirmation to see if anyone else was hearing what we heard. The third time you called, we noticed others who reacted in fear, and knew we were not the only ones who heard your call. Still riddled with echoes of the voices of the strangers we each followed, the third call of your name scared us, and we were all ready to leap into the P.O.N.R. Clubs for safety. Then you called your name the fourth time and it shook the Earth. The tremor caused Laughter, Tears and I to fall away from the doors of those clubs and into the arms of Remember, who carried us to safety with his friends. In this safety we were each given an opportunity to call ourselves back to ourselves, and we all did."

In a moment of great silence Love and Prayer knew they need not say another word. Prayer and Love hung up the phones with the same synchronicity they called one another with. All four of them had a four-day trip to get back to the park across from the restaurant. Like the experiences true relationships bring us, these experiences call us back after we discover there is nothing else that can offer us what we once had. Even if we let go of what truly matters, what truly matters never lets go of us.

On their four-day journeys back to the park across the street from the restaurant, Love was making her trek from a large city in the north. Prayer was voyaging from a small village in the east. Laughter was traveling from a small town in the south, and Tears was hiking from the west coast. Unlike the journeys away from one another they embarked upon many years ago, this journey was joyous. They each knew they were on a path to somewhere instead of nowhere. Throughout their individual journeys back to one another, they visited with the mad ones. And they each were looked at suspiciously by the masses but not fully rejected by them. The reactions of others no longer mattered. What did matter to each one of them were the memories of how things were when they were together. They traveled light, not much weighed them down, other than the occasional sight of someone walking into a P.O.N.R. Club as the individual ignored the pleadings from Remember. Those sightings were sad but important reminders they each almost made the fateful step inside the P.O.N.R. Club. Everything they never fulfilled but were supposed to, was dangerously close to being hung upon the walls of the alleys of All That Never Got to Be.

After four days of travel the Four neared the park at sundown. Love arrived first. Her great anticipation to be reunited with Prayer, Laughter and Tears made it possible for her to temporarily ignore the conditions of the park. Love walked through the archway of the park's entrance noticing the sign that held the name of the park was now dilapidated and barely visible. The park was desolate. The unrecognizable conditions of the once vibrant park that used to host nothing but life was shocking. Looking beyond the conditions of the park, Love looked for her best friends. One by one they began to show up. Prayer entered the park and ran into Love's embrace. Laughter came next, jumping up and down while embracing Love and Prayer. Tears arrived about a half hour later. His fatigue converted to a surge of energy when he was able to see his three best friends from a distance. He ran to them and they all shared an embrace they had longed for throughout the last four years. They all had sought this reunion in many things throughout their journeys, but it was not until this moment the void they had been seeking to fill vanished. All they missed and all that was missing from them returned when they returned to each other. For the first time in four years they held peace, not pieces.

The once vibrant park appeared desolate. Four years ago, the park was filled with grass so green it looked like a field of emeralds glistening in the sunlight; and flowers so vibrant they appeared as a rainbow streaking across the Earth. The Four sat down on the barren ground. For a moment, the Four were spellbound by all that had changed. The once amazing playground where the laughter of the children used to sing from was now reduced to a few rusted pieces buried in the hardened and cracked dirt. Perhaps within the remaining rusted pieces of swings and slides partly buried in the dirt, the songs of laughter from the children were buried as well. All their thoughts went to a great resurrection, and they each knew the others were thinking the same. Four years ago, the park was always filled with people day and night. But now it was only inhabited by a few who were obviously under the influences of numbing agents. Although they were all dismayed at how drastically things had changed for the worse, Love kept her focus on the truth, not the facts, which reminded the others to do the same. "Prayer told me you both met Remember and his friends as well," Love said to Laughter and Tears.

Joyously, Tears answered, "Yes, and I am very grateful we did. I am sure Prayer told you that we almost didn't, so thank you for calling yourself back to call us all back together. It was dangerously close for all of us. I don't want any of us to go through those things again."

"We won't," Laughter interjected, "Not as long as we stay together."

Stirred with confidence, Prayer said, "We will stay together. How could we drift apart after all we have been through?"

Tears thought for a moment and shared, "We did it once, so it's possible that we do it again."

Love beamed, "That can only happen if we forget. We all took a journey to find out what we are not, so we now know the truth of what we are. We have recommitted ourselves to ourselves and one another to live in a manner that makes forgetting unnecessary. I do not like that there is still residual doubt hanging around us from our separate journeys. It is coming out in the language we are using. I know the fire

28

purified me and melted away the calluses I had built up. Did all of you go through the same purification with Remember and his friends?"

"Yes. We all did," said Prayer. "I had many calluses as well, but fire wasn't used to purify me. I was on a mountain in a village when I almost went inside forever. Remember and his friends purified me with the air. I stood on the mountain with them. I allowed myself to feel the wind again. Of course, the wind was never absent, but my attention to it was. As it moved through the mountains and the trees, I allowed myself to hear its song again. It moved around me, upon me, and I breathed deeply for the first time in four years. Within the breath of life my breath began and is once more. I called my name and heard my song again as the wind carried me back to me."

"I was on the outskirts of a small town in a farm field," said Laughter. "Remember and his friends purified me with the Earth. I placed my hands and ear to the Earth. First, I heard what I had not listened to in four years, the Earth's heartbeat. After some time of listening, I felt my heart once again pulsate in rhythm with the Earth. I called out my name and within the rhythm of our heartbeats I was gently rocked out of my slumber and brought back to me."

"I was on the coast," Tears added. "Remember and his friends cleansed me with water. Standing on the shore of the beach I watched the waves coming toward me. With each wave I could see my reflection more clearly. As I stepped into the cold water it invigorated me. Although the tide was strong, it did not pull me under, it pulled me together. I stood in the water and continued to watch my reflection within the waves until I fully saw myself again. I called my name and the water returned it to me. The waves carried me back to me."

Curiously, Love asked, "So what's missing right now? Why are we experiencing a lag when we all know we are exactly where we are supposed to be? What is it we must do to complete what has begun with the help of Remember, Dreams, Vision and Purpose?"

Tears spoke up next. With an idea posed as a question that sounded good to all the grateful but weary travelers, Tears suggested, "It's dark now, and we all had a long four-day journey. Is it possible we are all just hungry and should go across the street to the restaurant and enjoy a good meal while we catch up?"

The suggestion of a great meal, celebrating the Four's permanent reunion at the same restaurant where they once separated four years ago received no argument from any of the Four. In unison, they stood up, and through their unified laughter exclaimed, "Excellent idea."

Love, Prayer, Laughter and Tears began to take the very short walk across the street from the park to the restaurant. Before crossing the street, they all paused at the curb, just staring at the restaurant they once knew. The Four were in complete shock at what they saw. A sloppily painted wooden sign hung above the entrance of the restaurant that read: P.O.N.R. Club. Above the sloppily painted sign remained the previous name of the restaurant, but only two letters from the restaurant's previous name were still lit, the Y and the H, and they were dim. The two remaining letters flickered weakly against the night sky. The entire name of the restaurant used to shine a beautiful, turquoise color that lit up the entire park for all to enjoy any time of day or night. "What are we supposed to do now?" exclaimed Laughter. "These places are popping up all over. After everything we have been through, I'm not going in there."

"You're right, *you* are not going in there, *we* are going in there," insisted Love with a determination she had not felt in years.

"Are you crazy?" Prayer questioned, "We all nearly lost ourselves forever inside those hideous clubs."

"Exactly," agreed Tears, "You were the one who helped us call ourselves back so we wouldn't end up in a place like that. Now you want to call us into the same place you called us away from? Are you even listening to yourself, Love?"

"Yes. For the first time in four years I am listening to myself. Even though I cannot clearly explain it yet, I know we have to go in there. We must do this together. Look at the park. Look at the restaurant. Look at us not being in a flow like we used to be with one another. We must take this all the way. I trust my voice. I trust the process. I know we need to do this, and we have to do this together."

Although Love was unable to provide an explanation to the others, the others knew Love, and knew that explanations were not always possible or necessary with her. Following the certainty of Love, they agreed to enter the P.O.N.R. Club together. Crossing the street, the Four took notice of four very large men standing in front of the entrance staring at them. They were not saying anything to the Four, but they were not excusing themselves as the Four attempted to enter. "Excuse us," said Love, knowing there was about to be a confrontation.

"You Four are not welcome here. You can't go in," said the four large men in unison.

"Why can't we go in?" Love asked.

The four burly men, laughing and looking down at the Four, said, "For many reasons. Let's just say we have a color code at this club, and we don't allow your kind here."

Calmly, Love replied, "All of us are colorless, and yet are made up of every color known and unknown to humankind."

The four large men looked at each other and began laughing more loudly. One of them, in a much more menacing tone sneered, "We are the reasons you can't get in and we'll just leave it at that." Love recalled something familiar about these men, but she did not know exactly what it was. With a quick change in attitude, one of the four menacing men looked at Love and offered, "Okay, we'll let you through, but only one at a time."

Love reached out and held Prayer's hand, Prayer reached to Laughter, and Laughter reached to Tears. Once that connection was made with them and within them, Love remembered exactly how she knew the four burly men. They were the voice she heard four years ago that told her she was vulnerable and needed to become invulnerable. They were the voice she listened to that took her far away from who she is, almost losing herself forever. Holding tightly to the hands of her best friends she asked, "Who are you?"

In unison they hissed, "We are Doubt."

Gripping even more tightly to her friend's hand, and with her voice trembling, Love said, "I…I remember you."

Amused by the trembling in Love's voice, Doubt yelled, "We told you that you were vulnerable. Listen to you stutter. Have you learned nothing?" The treacherous laughter from Doubt grew louder as it echoed through the streets, against the walls of the restaurant and into the park.

Quickly, Love recalled the things she experienced with Remember so she remembered herself and what the Four are together. Never letting go of the hands of her friends, Love looked Doubt in the eyes and avowed, "I said I remember you, and from time to time in the future I may remember you again, but I will never again forget me or my friends. From now on, every time I remember you it will only cause me to remember who I am even more intensely. I followed your voice and discovered everything I am not. In this discovery I have come back to myself and my friends even stronger. We are entering this place together and there is nothing you can do about it. I am Love."

As soon as Love declared her name to herself and Doubt, the menacing, husky men transformed to small shadows that could do nothing but scurry away, screaming in the agony of defeat Love had brought them by affirming herself. There was no time for celebration. The Four knew they were on a mission. The awareness of what they learned apart from one another and how it could now benefit them together was unfolding. Together they stepped through the front door and into the P.O.N.R. Club. The door quickly shut behind them and a predictable stench filled the air. It took a moment for their eyes to adjust to the dimly lit establishment. What was immediately visible to the Four was a digital clock above the podium where there used to be a host to seat the patrons. In bright red letters the clock continuously flashed: *It's Too Late for You.*

The Four noticed that no one was sitting together. Everyone was in solitude. Within the restaurant, every type of numbing agent imaginable was on all the tables. Some of the numbing agents were the ones that provide temporary relief immediately; others were the ones that provide immediate relief permanently. The only people sitting together were in the very back table on the left-hand side of the club. Love, Prayer, Laughter and Tears recognized that it was the owner, You. The Four had known You their entire childhood and most of their adolescence. Sitting with You was a woman who had her back to the Four, but the Four noticed she was dressed the same as Doubt. The Four waved to You. With a look of surprise and concern seeing the Four in what was now a P.O.N.R. Club, You replied with a polite nod, but You quickly gave every ounce of attention You had back to the woman sitting at the table. The woman who had the complete attention of You turned around and looked at the Four with a condescending smirk, shook her head with contempt, then turned back around and continued to speak to You.

The Four made their way past what used to be the host station and into the dining room. They passed the many people sitting alone at the tables whose only company were the numbing agents. The Four found the same round table in the middle of the dining room they used to meet and eat at every day. There was only one chair at the large round table, so Laughter grabbed three other chairs from a nearby table. Before the Four sat down, with evident irritation, and in one swift motion, Tears wiped the table clear of the numbing agents that were piled in the middle of their table. Several people scurried to the numbing agents on the floor, picked them up and ran back to their individual tables. After Love, Prayer, Laughter and Tears sat down at their table, a waiter and his three assistants greeted the Four, "Hello. What can we get you this evening?"

Before Love could order first, the woman sitting with You commanded the waiter and his assistants, "Give them the works. It's on me. No worries tonight. I will take care of all of you."

Shockingly to everyone, You yelled, "Don't accept anything and especially don't eat anything from here." The woman laughed, leaned in toward You and whispered. Whatever she whispered made You slouch back in the chair in what looked to be complete defeat.

Receiving instructions from the woman, the waiter and his assistants went to the kitchen and quickly returned to the table. Each of them carried a plate covered with a silver lid. The waiter and his assistants stood between Love, Prayer, Laughter and Tears, not with them. The waiter and his assistants smoothly placed the entrées on the table in front of each of the Four. In unison, the waiter and his assistants leaned in, placed their hands upon the silver lids, but before they unveiled the meals, they began to whisper to the Four. The waiter whispered in Love's ear, "You are fragile. You are weak and too sensitive. You need to go back out and complete your journey to find real strength." Repeatedly the waiter continued to say this to Love, never taking his hand off the silver lid, and never taking his lips away from Love's ear.

The same thing was happening to the others. One assistant was whispering in Prayer's ear, "You're not realistic. You do not work. Your words are impotent in a deaf universe. Go back out and finish your journey in finding out how to be useful."

Another assistant whispered to Laughter, "You are unsophisticated. You are immature. You know nothing about the real world and how to be successful in it. You are an irritant to those who truly understand. Go back out and finish your lesson in how to become polished, put-together, and important."

The assistant who whispered to Tears was the most vicious of them all. The assistant oppressively hissed to Tears, "You are ready to let them out right now, aren't you? You know why? Because you are weak. You are just prey in a world that does not want you. With every tear you have ever let out it only brought you more pain, more agony to endure. Your so-called friends only keep you along for the ride because they feel sorry for you. They do not want you. They do not need you. And they surely do not respect you."

The frenzied whispers continued in all forms of hurt and deception imaginable and unimaginable. At the same time, never ceasing their whispers, the waiter and his assistants lifted the silver lids from the plates. The food that was unveiled to each of the Four looked vile and the smell was equally unpleasant. Even though the Four were sitting next to one another, the continued whispers from the waiter and his assistants began to make them feel miles apart. The more they listened to the whispers, the less disgusting the food smelled and appeared. Each plate contained equal, double portions of dis-ease, dissatisfaction, disconnectedness, unforgiveness, guilt, blame and regret, all covered in the thick P.O.N.R. Club specialty sauce, terror. As this process unfolded, the woman at the table with You looked on in extreme pleasure as You wept. You had seen this many times before. You knew if the Four consumed that food, that food would certainly consume them and create an appetite for the numbing agents so insatiable the Four would soon be at separate tables and never find their way out of the P.O.N.R. Club.

Amidst the frenzied whispers of the waiter and his assistants, other softer whispers began to rise. With each passing moment they increased in volume and strength. "I am Love." "I am Prayer." "I am Laughter." "I am Tears." As the Four reminded themselves of who they were individually, they reached out to one another underneath the table that had upon it an offering of everything they are not. Connected hand in hand, the Four began to remind one another who they are together. Seeing the Four had connected hand in hand, the woman sitting with You jumped out of her seat and screamed, "No!" You looked on in amazement and became filled with something You had not felt since the Four's last meal at the restaurant, hope. As the Four in unison repeated their holy names to themselves and one another, they raised one another's hands high above the table. With the Four now having their hands connected and fully extended upward, their voices blended in a powerful, sacred union. The places on this Earth where you can still participate in the great awakening every morning was brought within the P.O.N.R. Club by the Four. Like sunrise on a pristine beach, the Four's unification ascended like the fire from the rising sun blending with the still waters of the sea, as the Breath of creation carries the sacred elements throughout the Earth, causing all life to be. The Four's unified voice drowned out the voices of the waiter and his assistants. The waiter and his assistants were repelled from the table where they fell silent. At the peak of this moment, holding one another's hands in a circle that should have never been broken, Love, Prayer, Laughter and Tears became silent as well. A look of relief came upon the woman who had held the attention of You captive for so long. Looking up at the table from the floor, the waiter and his assistants smirked with a perceived sense of victory. A look of disappointment overtook You. Although misperceived by everyone else, the Four understood this moment. Misperceptions have nothing to do with the truth of the Four. Within this great silence, the Four's unification was complete with a certainty beyond pronunciation or proclamation. A certainty that is within every truth allowed to be unveiled and is what unveils every truth. Thinking this moment of silence was a moment of weakness for the Four, the woman sitting with You decided to proclaim her name. Loudly she screamed, "I am Lies." Always taking her lead, the waiter announced his name yelling, "I am Fear." One by one, the waiter's assistants announced, "I am Fear." "I am Fear." "I am Fear." No matter its form or its various names, a lie always lies in fear and fear always lies in lies. They all come from the same place and when listened to, lead to the same place - nowhere. Continuing to hold each others' hands high above the table, the Four remained silent while Fear and Lies screamed in a last-ditch effort to deceive. But this time the Four did not let go of one another. They were no longer going to follow the voices of strangers. They stayed true to their truth. Their unified, sacred truth holds all the questions and answers, as well as the road to peace. Their time apart prepared them for this moment. They now knew, not merely believed, they were each the piece that pieces peace together. Love gave all of herself to Prayer, Prayer gave all of himself to Laughter, Laughter gave all of herself to Tears, and now

41

Tears was able to give all of himself. It was within Tears that Love, Prayer and Laughter manifested into one. Love loved, Prayer prayed, Laughter laughed and the tears from Tears were no longer weak, but strong, because they were flowing. As the first tears from Tears landed upon the table, the food offered to the Four immediately transformed to forgiveness, compassion, empathy, generosity, faith, hope and peace. When the horrid foods that were offered to the Four transformed to a beautiful meal, Lies and Fear became so filled with themselves they fled the restaurant screaming. A torrent of tears continued to pour through Tears and quickly flooded the P.O.N.R. Club. The life-giving purification rained from Tears and dissolved the numbing agents and every other abhorrent ingredient that accompanied Lies and Fear into the restaurant four years ago. Awestruck, the individuals who were all at separate tables were now gathered together, staring at beautiful plates of food in front of them that were once numbing agents. A thunderous wave of tears slammed the front door of the restaurant open and knocked down the sloppily painted P.O.N.R. Club sign onto the street where it disintegrated down into the sewer. The stream of purification flooded the park across the street. Nothing remained in the restaurant except the beauty that was there four years ago before the Four separated. Drenched in the rain of purification, the eyes of You shone like a newborn child. You could now see with a clarity only an awakening of the Four can provide. You ran up to the table of miracles where Love, Prayer, Laughter and Tears sat. "Thank you so much," exclaimed You. You embraced them all with a hug. Love, Prayer, Laughter and Tears were just staring at You in an inquisitive and playful manner.

"What is it?" You asked.

Tears divulged, "Before Lies and her staff were washed out of here for good, she left this." Tears handed You the deed to the restaurant You signed over to Lies shortly after the Four parted ways four years ago.

Happily, You asked, "I thought she got the deed transferred to her name?"

Lovingly, Love shared, "There is no choice for Lies other than to give it all back when we are all together."

United, the Four purified the restaurant and severed the chains Lies and Fear held You captive with. The restaurant was returned to its former glory, making it suitable to give back to You. It was once again a place of refuge, providing the nourishment, purity, truth and peace it did years ago. You sat down with the Four, not between them. Gazing around the room they watched the patrons laughing and eating together. Tears exclaimed, "Okay, let's eat." The Four and

You filled themselves with the blessed food, conversation and a presence that nourished them mentally, physically, spiritually and emotionally. After hours of indulging in their unified goodness they sat back with smiles, soaking in the long-awaited new beginning. Something caught the attention of You and the Four. One by one they all looked toward the front window of the restaurant. They were all hearing familiar sounds they had not heard in four years. You and the Four walked to the window and saw they were indeed hearing what they had hoped for. From the window they observed the park was once again filled with people. The laughter of the children was so strong it vibrated the windows of the restaurant. The children were playing on the resurrected swings and slides that looked like they had just been built. The once downtrodden users of numbing agents who were lying in the park just hours ago, were now drinking the waters of purification that flooded the park and were smiling. Underneath the four inches of water, the once dried-out, hardened dirt had transformed back to grass so green it looked like a field of emeralds glistening in the moonlight. People were dancing in the waters of purification and running around the park. Even the huge sign that held the name of the park on the archway entrance was revitalized by the purification of the Four. The excitement was more than the Four could stand but exactly what they all wanted to stand within. Love exclaimed, "We have plenty to sing, paint, write and draw. Let's get over there and join them in this great dance of gratitude."

Like children, not wanting to miss a moment of joy life has to offer, they quickly walked out of the restaurant to join everyone. While crossing the street, You and the Four gazed in wonderment at the revitalized sign on the archway of the park's entrance which once again, in beautiful golden letters read: *The World*. The World was restored to life by the purification that comes from the great courage only existent within the Four.

You and the Four crossed through the archway of the World and joined in the great gratitude of peace that had occurred. In a whirlwind of joy led by the Four, everyone was playing, laughing, singing, dancing, writing and painting. Welcomed once more, Remember, Purpose, Dreams and Vision ran out of the alley of All That Never Got to Be and joined everyone in the World. Amidst the celebration of this great renewal, the children were the first to notice yet another miracle unfolding in front of everyone in the World. One by one, the children stopped what they were doing, and their eyes were captivated by what they saw across the street from the World. The Four, along with everyone else in the World, began to take notice. They all gazed across the street in amazement along with the children. It was another sight that no one thought they would ever see again. Once again, lighting up the evening with the beautiful turquoise light, was the name of the restaurant. The light shone so bright it blended with the stars and cast beams of light upon not just the eyes of the onlookers, but upon their souls as well. The only one in the park not taking notice was You. You was splashing around in the waters of purification near the playground, laughing a belly laugh You had not heard, felt or enjoyed in four years. Love called out to You. Laughing and still not taking notice of the hundreds of people in silence staring at the restaurant under You's care, You walked up to Love and exclaimed, "This is great. The Four are back together. The park is beautiful again. The children are laughing. Everyone is singing, painting, drawing, writing and dancing. Thank you all so much. I don't know how all this happened, but I am so grateful it did."

Love smiled upon You, "Look around for a moment because everyone in the World is beholding how this happened."

You paused, looked around, and now became fully aware everyone in the World was gazing in a sacred silence in the same direction. As You looked in the direction everyone else was, You was overcome with awe. With reverential gratitude, You observed the once nearly burned out sign that carried the name of the restaurant had been brought back to life. The rejuvenated sign is more than just a sign, it is the answer. An answer not found in questions but found within the certainty of Love, Prayer, Laughter and Tears. In a beautiful, turquoise light the name of the restaurant once again illuminated the park, danced across the waters of purification, and reflected in the eyes of everyone in the World. Cleansed and renewed, placed back in the hands of You and flooding the World with all its goodness, *Your Heart* is once again open.

www.realwarriorslove.com

Made in the USA
Monee, IL
04 November 2023

45678493R00036